The
Keyboard Kitten

An Oregon Children's Story

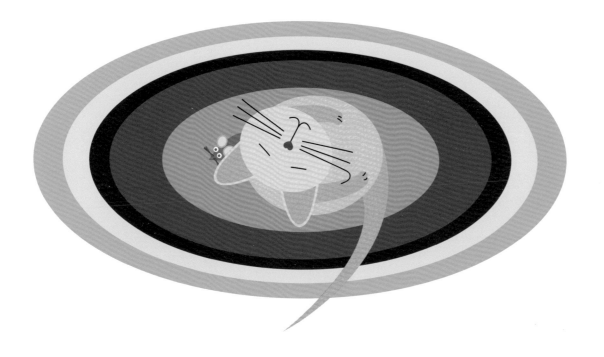

Story by
BOB WELCH

Illustrations by
TOM PENIX

NIMROD · JUNCTION CITY · DRAIN   **penwax**design   MIST · CHRISTMAS VALLEY · ECHO

Published by penwaxdesign

ISBN: 978-0-9883329-2-8

Printed in Canada

Keyboard Kitten website: www.keyboardkitten.com

To contact author Bob Welch: info@bobwelch.net

To contact illustrator Tom Penix: tompenix@gmail.com

*To loved ones, past and present, who, like us, take their humor seriously.
Thanks for believing in us, encouraging us, and putting up with us.*

On a wet Oregon morn, Matt awakened to write
Shuffled into the kitchen and flicked on the light
Opened his laptop, filled the teapot anew
And, half asleep, waited for his cocoa to brew

All asleep, in one corner, lay a small ball of fur
A two-month-old kitten, not a "him" but a "her"
She dreamed of writing stories with a's, b's, and c's
Although all Matt could hear now was unending zzz's

Matt had written for years and not tasted success
But kept writing his children's book nevertheless
About an Oregon boy with a talent quite rare:
When rain fell in buckets he could swim through the air

Matt called his book *Rain Boy* and each morning awoke
To write in a house dwarfed by fir, pine, and oak
He dreamed of when *Rain Boy* would one day be through
And draw praise in a *Register-Guard* book review

Children would read Matt's story and laugh with delight
Their imaginations soaring like high-flying kites
From Yachats to Vale, Matt would be much in demand
And he would take his family to Disneyland

In real life, Matt's confidence sank terribly low
And he felt stuck in the muck with nowhere to go
"I'm a failure," he heard his inner-child mutter
While Oregon's liquid sunshine dripped from the gutter

In defeat, Matt bowed his head to whisper a prayer
While the teapot steam softened his sleep-crumpled hair
He stared at the screen and thought, "What can I do?"
When he heard the soft sound of a kitty-cat's mew

She arched her back with a slight sense of drama
'Twas the once-sleeping cat, a kitten called Comma
Named for the shape in which she would sleepily curl
When not causing chaos in some hurricane swirl

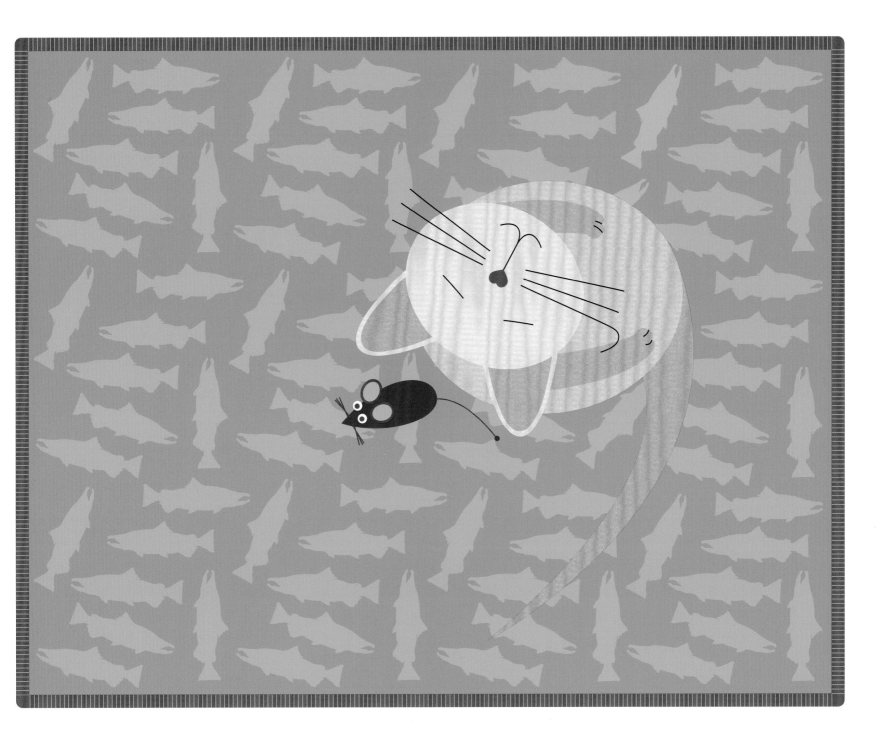

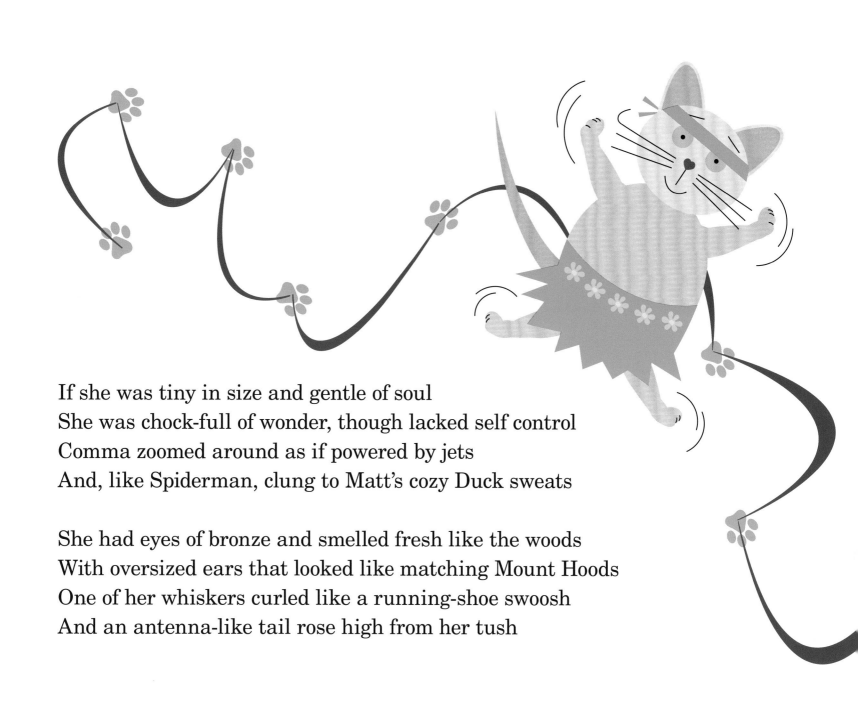

If she was tiny in size and gentle of soul
She was chock-full of wonder, though lacked self control
Comma zoomed around as if powered by jets
And, like Spiderman, clung to Matt's cozy Duck sweats

She had eyes of bronze and smelled fresh like the woods
With oversized ears that looked like matching Mount Hoods
One of her whiskers curled like a running-shoe swoosh
And an antenna-like tail rose high from her tush

Comma crawled on Matt's shoulders not one time but twice
Then pounced on his hands like they were enemy mice
In no mood to play, Matt brushed Comma aside
But she was back in a flash to toy with his pride

To protect his kingdom, Matt stacked books up so high
That there appeared no way a cat could get by
But when gently pushed back with a light-handed bop
Comma jumped the book-wall with the Fosbury Flop

Day after day, Comma continued to pester
Matt wasn't about to continue to test her
Night after night, the kitten crept into Matt's dreams
As a meowing monster scheming new schemes

Whatever Matt dreamed of — *The Lorax* or llamas
It was lost in a parade of five hundred Commas
He dreamt of New York in chocolate and vanilla
Stalked by a kitten twice the size of Godzilla

Like clogged ice from a Dari Mart fountain machine
Matt's words froze in his mind, with few reaching his screen
He poured some granola, and sliced Tillamook cheese
While Comma cat-napped atop the sixty-eight keys

When she pranced from A to L with hardly a care
Matt feared she might let loose and cried, "Please, don't you dare!"
Too late — she started to squat with obvious glee
But fooled Matt by just pressing the key marked with "P"

PPPPPPPPP P

To escape his foe, Matt moved from kitchen to den
And when no Comma showed up, he called it "win-win"
But as he wrestled with words lacking zippity-zap
He felt Comma the kitten crawl onto his lap

Too tired for battle, Matt leaned back in despair
And watched Comma hop to his desk from the chair
She marched down the keyboard like a majestic queen
The results popping up on the computer's screen

B *
S r
@
T E
T
m

"Rain Boy"

Trees

Yellow hair

Orange trunks

"Now you've done it, Comma, you've garbled my story
I can forget about best sellers and book-writing glory
You've ruined *Rain Boy* and all that I've worked towards
Goodbye fame, fortune, and Oregon Book Awards"

Then Matt's eyes grew wide, for what he saw was absurd
The paws of Ms. Comma were creating real words
That when linked like the cars of the Coast Starlight train
Formed sentences as on track as those of Mark Twain

To do
1. Up by 5:30
2. Finish book
3. Hide from
4. Family time
5. Save for Dis

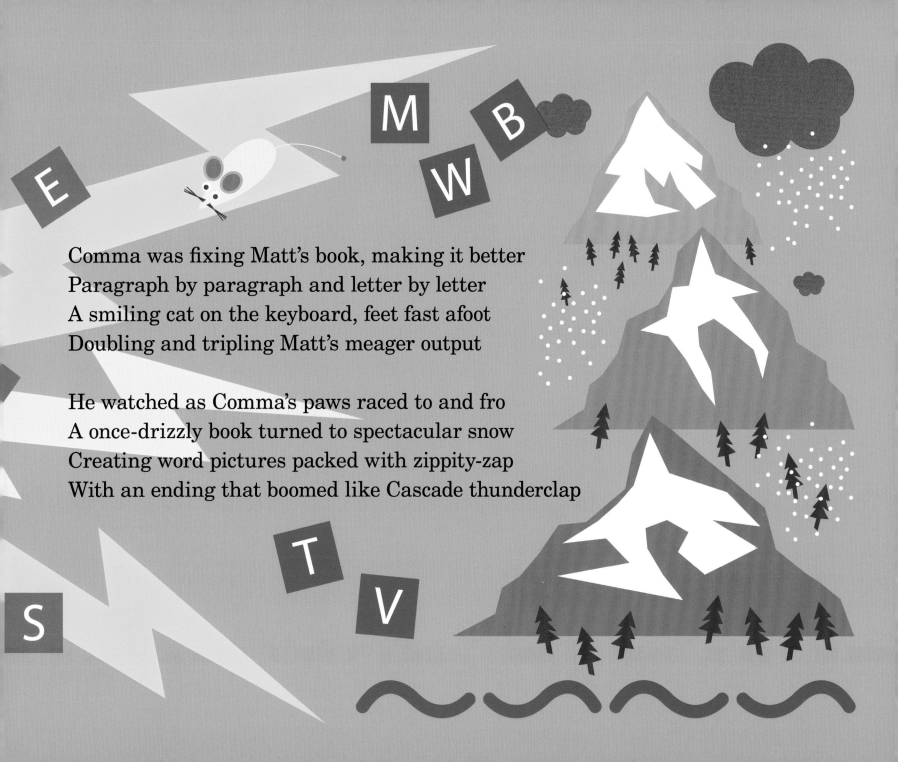

Comma was fixing Matt's book, making it better
Paragraph by paragraph and letter by letter
A smiling cat on the keyboard, feet fast afoot
Doubling and tripling Matt's meager output

He watched as Comma's paws raced to and fro
A once-drizzly book turned to spectacular snow
Creating word pictures packed with zippity-zap
With an ending that boomed like Cascade thunderclap

The bewhiskered young writer then casually stopped
Licked her paws, washed her face, then down the cat hopped
Matt's wonder gave way to a slight sense of sorrow
Till he saw Comma's last words: "Same time tomorrow?"

Humbled, Matt showed up, not the least bit upset
To join a cat he realized was far more than a pet
They took turns at the keyboard, crafting their tale
Taking it from dockside to full-Fern-Ridge-Lake sail

At Last

Day after day, the odd couple worked as a team
Fixing not only *Rain Boy* but Matt's self-esteem
When the book was published, they awaited reviews
And both were elated when they learned of the news

Children read Matt's story and laughed with delight
Their imaginations soaring like high-flying kites
From Yachats to Vale, Matt was much in demand
And, yep, he took his family to Disneyland

On the Peter Pan ride, a cool moment occurred
A high-five exchange as Comma happily purred
Matt and the cat, sharing a ship through the sky
Celebrating as authors in matching tie-dye

Back home in Oregon, the two launched a new book
Inspired by a note left on Matt's newly bought Nook:
"We need one another," Matt saw she had written
"More adventures to come! Love, The Keyboard Kitten"

Oregon Glossary

A little help for our younger readers and those not familiar with our state

Cascade thunderclap: Crash of thunder in the Cascade Mountains.

Coast Starlight Train: Amtrak passenger train that runs through Oregon, from Seattle to Los Angeles.

Dari Mart: Chain of nearly four dozen convenience stores from Albany to Cottage Grove, locally owned by the Gibson family of Junction City since 1965.

Duck sweats: University of Oregon sweatpants.

Fern Ridge Lake: One of Oregon's best sailing lakes, located just west of Eugene.

Granola: Breakfast and snack food, popular in Eugene, made of rolled oats, nuts, honey, and sometimes puffed rice.

Fosbury Flop: High-jump style invented in the early 1960s by Dick Fosbury, who attended Medford High and Oregon State University — and, in 1968, won an Olympic gold medal.

Liquid sunshine: Slang term for Oregon's rain.

Mount Hood: At 11,249 feet, Oregon's highest mountain. Located 50 miles east of Portland.

Oregon Book Awards: Honors given each year to the state's finest writers.

The Register-Guard: Oregon's second-largest daily newspaper.

Running-shoe swoosh: Reference to the "swoosh" on shoes made by Nike, located in Beaverton.

Tie-dye: Process of tying and dyeing a piece of fabric or cloth, often into bright, swirling colors. Particularly popular in Eugene in the 1960s.

Tillamook cheese: Cheese made at a company that's been operating for more than 100 years in a small town on Oregon's northern coast.

Vale: Town twelve miles from the Oregon-Idaho border. Not as far east as Ontario, but what rhymes with Ontario?

Yachats: Small village on the central Oregon coast. Pronounced YAH-hots, though some newcomers say YATCH-itz.

More adventures to come!
— Love, The Keyboard Kitten